Jellybean Books™

Which Witch Is Which?

By Michaela Muntean
Illustrated by
Tom Brannon

Featuring
Jim Henson's
Sesame Street
Muppets

Copyright © 1996 Children's Television Workshop (Sesame Street Muppets © 1996 The Jim Henson Company. All rights reserved under International and Pan-American Copyright Conventions. Published in the United States by Random House, Inc., New York, and simultaneously in Canada by Random House of Canada Limited, Toronto, in conjunction with Children's Television Workshop. Sesame Street, the Sesame Street sign, and CTW books are trademarks and service marks of Children's Television Workshop. Originally published by Golden Books Publishing Company, Inc., in 1996. First Random House edition, 1999.
Library of Congress Catalog Number: 99-070249
ISBN 0-375-80385-8

www.randomhouse.com/kids
www.sesamestreet.com

Printed in the United States of America 10 9 8 7 6 5 4 3 2 1
RANDOM HOUSE and colophon are registered trademarks of Random House, Inc.
JELLYBEAN BOOKS and colophon are trademarks of Random House, Inc.

"**L**isten, everybody," said Zoe. "I have a terrific idea for our Halloween costumes. Let's all go dressed as witches!"

"It'll be the 'trick' part of 'trick or treat,'" she explained. "No one will be able to tell *which witch is which!*"

Zoe, Elmo, Telly, Grover, and Herry worked
hard on their costumes. They made long black
capes and pointy hats. They found frizzy fright
wigs, warty noses, and, of course, some brooms.

On Halloween, five witches set out to go trick-or-treating.
Their first stop was the lobby of the Furry Arms Hotel.

"Trick or treat!" said one of the witches. "Guess which witch is Grover."

Sherry Netherland pointed to one of the witches. "Is it you?"

"No!" cried the five witches.

"Well, you sure tricked me," said Sherry, and she gave each of them a candied apple.

The elephant elevator operator couldn't guess which witch was Telly.

So he gave each of the witches a bag of peanuts.

Up and down Sesame Street went the five witches.
At every stop they tried their trick, but no one could
guess which witch was Telly...

or Grover...

or Zoe...

or Elmo...

or Herry.

Their trick-or-treat bags were getting heavier and heavier.

"This is the best Halloween ever," said Zoe, and she spun around, swirling her long black cape.

Herry and Telly laughed in a cackling, witchy way.

Elmo and Grover pretended they were riding their brooms.

Their next stop was Oscar's trash can.

"Trick!" they cried.

Oscar peered out from under his trash can lid.

"What kind of trick?" he asked suspiciously.

"Guess which witch is Herry," said the five witches. "That's easy," said Oscar. "Let me see your feet." Oscar guessed that the witch with the big blue feet was Herry.

"Grover is the one with the little blue feet," he said. "Bright pink feet? That has to be Telly. The one with little red feet could only be Elmo. That leaves one witch with orange feet, which must belong to Zoe."

"You're right," said the five witches.

"Of course I'm right," said Oscar. "Grouches are grouchy, not stupid. Now I don't have to give you a treat."

"Aw, come on, Oscar," complained the five witches.

"Grumble all you want," said Oscar. "It's music to my ears! Just remember that it's trick *or* treat, not trick *and* treat."

"You're right again," the five witches said sadly, and they began to walk away.

"Okay—wait!" Oscar called after them. "Because I'm such a bighearted grouch, I've changed my mind."

He disappeared inside his trash can and returned
a minute later with a platter of little sandwiches.
"Here's your treat," he said, "but first I have a
trick for *you*. Guess which sandwich is which."

"Do you have peanut butter and jelly?" asked the
witch with the little red feet. "That is Elmo's favorite."

"No," said Oscar, "but I do have chocolate and tuna fish, sardine and garlic, and eggplant and prune." "Yucch!" said the five witches.

"What's the matter?" asked Oscar. "I thought witches would like sand*wiches* for a treat."

"Well," said Zoe, "I guess this time the *trick* is on us!"